27 July 2000 ~

FOR All The Children of TaunTon
I hope you have as much
Fun reading This as I had
painting it!
enjoy!

Hello Willow

By Kimberly Poulton

Illustrated by Jennifer O'Keefe

Moon Mountain
PUBLISHING

North Kingstown, Rhode Island

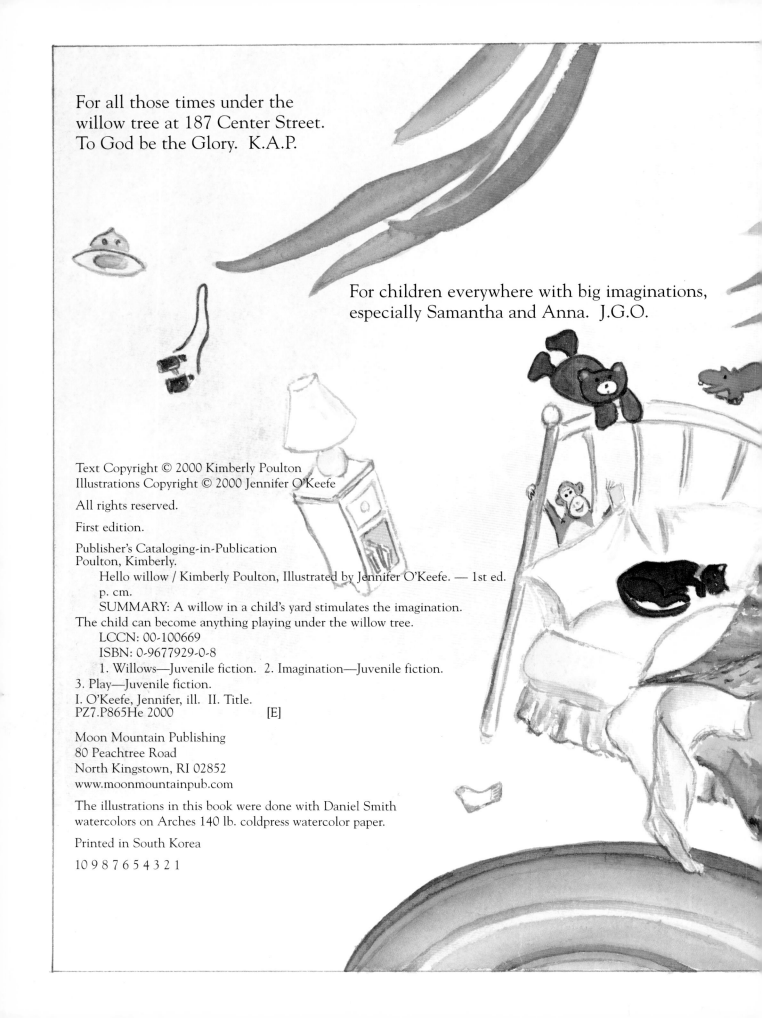

For all those times under the
willow tree at 187 Center Street.
To God be the Glory. K.A.P.

For children everywhere with big imaginations,
especially Samantha and Anna. J.G.O.

Text Copyright © 2000 Kimberly Poulton
Illustrations Copyright © 2000 Jennifer O'Keefe

All rights reserved.

First edition.

Publisher's Cataloging-in-Publication
Poulton, Kimberly.
    Hello willow / Kimberly Poulton, Illustrated by Jennifer O'Keefe. — 1st ed.
    p. cm.
    SUMMARY: A willow in a child's yard stimulates the imagination.
The child can become anything playing under the willow tree.
    LCCN: 00-100669
    ISBN: 0-9677929-0-8
    1. Willows—Juvenile fiction. 2. Imagination—Juvenile fiction.
3. Play—Juvenile fiction.
I. O'Keefe, Jennifer, ill. II. Title.
PZ7.P865He 2000   [E]

Moon Mountain Publishing
80 Peachtree Road
North Kingstown, RI 02852
www.moonmountainpub.com

The illustrations in this book were done with Daniel Smith
watercolors on Arches 140 lb. coldpress watercolor paper.

Printed in South Korea

10 9 8 7 6 5 4 3 2 1

Hello
Willow

I have a willow tree in my yard.

It greets me with a wave at my window
each morning.

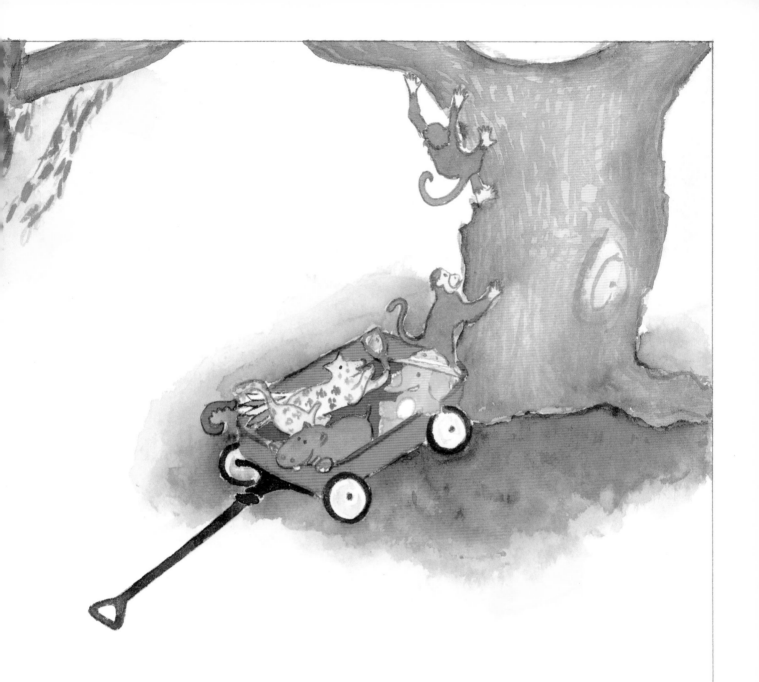

I love to play underneath its soft, green
branches that fall to the ground
like long feathers.

I can be a monkey in the jungle swinging from branch to branch.

I can be a fearless explorer on safari, waiting to spot just the right animal or bird.

Sometimes I pretend I'm a hairdresser and
tie the branches up like braids
or give myself a long, flowing wig.

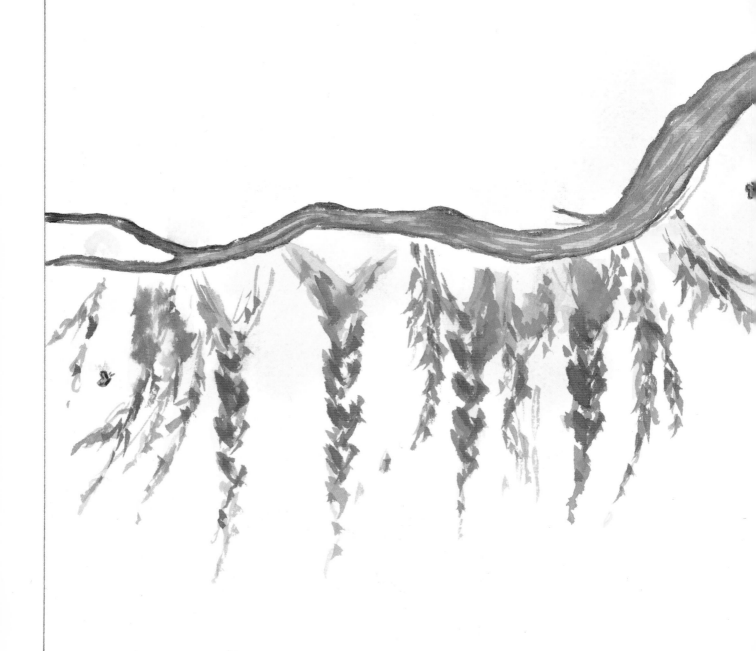

Or I am a caterpillar
wrapping myself up in a cocoon
soon to become a butterfly.

On hot days, it's a great spot for a picnic in the shade with my friends.

When it rains, I do not worry because
I have my own big umbrella.

It is very useful for sweeping or dusting when
I want to play house.

And it's a great place to play hide-and-seek.

Sometimes I am happy just to curl up against its big, strong trunk and take a nap.

But not for long, because soon I am awake with a tickle at my nose!

When it's time to go, I
politely shake each branch
and say,

"Thank you for a
wonderful day. I'll see you
in the morning!"

Do you suppose that willow trees sleep?

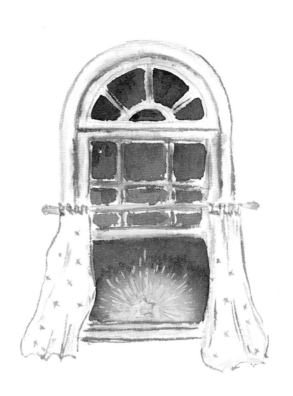